DISNEY

the Never Girls

THE GRAPHIC NOVEL

THE ART of FRIENDSHIP

DISNEY PUBLISHING WORLDWIDE

GLOBAL MAGAZINES, COMICS, AND PARTWORKS

PUBLISHER
Lynn Waggoner

EXECUTIVE EDITOR
Carlotta Quattrocolo

EDITORIAL TEAM
Bianca Coletti (Director, Magazines), Guido
Frazzini (Director, Comics), Stefano Ambrosio
(Executive Editor), Camilla Vedove (Senior
Manager, Editorial Development),
Behnoosh Khalili (Senior Editor), Julie Dorris
(Senior Editor), Kendall Tamer (Assistant Editor),
Cristina Casas (Assistant Editor)

DESIGN
Enrico Soave (Senior Designer)

ART
Ken Shue (VP, Global Art),
Roberto Santillo (Creative Director),
Manny Mederos (Senior Illustration Manager),
Marco Ghiglione (Creative Manager),
Stefano Attardi (Illustration Manager)

PORTFOLIO MANAGEMENT
Olivia Ciancarelli (Director)

BUSINESS & MARKETING
Mariantonietta Galla
(Senior Manager, Franchise),
Virpi Korhonen (Editorial Manager)

Random House 🏠 New York

rhcbooks.com

ISBN 978-0-7364-4396-8 (trade) — ISBN 978-0-7364-4397-5 (ebook) —
ISBN 978-0-7364-9039-9 (lib. bdg.)

Printed in the United States of America

10 9 8 7 6 5 4 3 2 1

DISNEP
The NeVeR GiRls
THE GRAPHIC NOVEL

THE ART OF FRIENDSHIP

Written by Sloane Leong

Art by Kawaii Creative Studio

Design and lettering by Chris Dickey

Based on the chapter book
series by Kiki Thorpe

The Story of the Never Girls

The directions are simple. It's the second star to the right, and straight on till morning.

But sometimes you don't need directions, only the belief in your heart that magic is real.

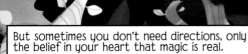

Clap if you believe in magic!

CLAP CLAP

One day, in their own backyard, four special girls found a portal...

...to a special place!

NEVER LAND

Meet the Never Girls

Mia Vasque[z]

Mia adores beautiful and fanciful things. She is Kate's best frie[nd] and Gabby's loving o[lder] sister. Mia is curious, adventurous, and helpful to her friends [in] both her world and in Never Land.

Kate McCrady

Kate is always ready for an exciting adventure! She's sporty and loves to play soccer. Though sometimes overconfident, Kate is a strong leader and a trusted friend.

Lainey Winters

Lainey loves animals. She's talkative and dreams of being able to chat with her animal friends! Though Lainey is often lost in her own world, she's a thoughtful and loyal friend.

Gabby Vasquez

Gabby is Mia's little sister and the youngest of the four Never Girls. She is playful and imaginative. Gabby likes to wear a pair of wings, pretending to be one of her favorite things: a fairy.

Meet the Fairies

Cadence

Cadence is a music-talent fairy who loves to play instruments, especially the drums. She's creative, curious, and inspiring, and she knows just how to help when the Never Girls need it.

Leo

Leo is an art-talent sparrow man who enjoys drawing and painting pictures of his environment in Never Land. He is known for creating large, colorful murals. Leo uses his artistic talents to inspire others, which makes him an excellent art teacher.

Chapter 1
Boom in Bloom

On a beautiful day in Never Land, Leo is painting pictures of butterflies...

BOOM

Meanwhile...

Okay, next question: What's your favorite type of weather?

Stormy! Because the rain and thunder sound like drums. It's like the sky is making music.

I never thought about it like that!

Chapter 2
Billy the New Kid

...go!

You've gotta be faster than that!

w are
ou so
uick?!

Practice! And soon you'll be as fast as me.

Soon you'll be too fast for this mean kid to even *see*!

Haha!

Chapter 3
Giving Space

The next day...

RIIIING

BILLY

Chapter 4
Trolled

The next day...

RIIIING

All right, time for lunch! When you're back, I'll be collecting your drawings from last week.

Oh no! Where's my sketchboo

Oh no! Leo!

Girls?

What happened, Leo?

Leech. Leech did this.

Oh no, your painting!

Why would he do this!

Leech can't get away with this. Let's go talk to him.

I didn't think you'd like my drawings. I didn't think you liked... me.

I get that.

Yeah, I can get shy sometimes, too.

Humph.

How about you help me fix the mural, and we'll call it even, okay?

Really?

Yes! Adding trolls is going to make it very unique, I think.

I'd like that.

Chapter 5
The Invitation

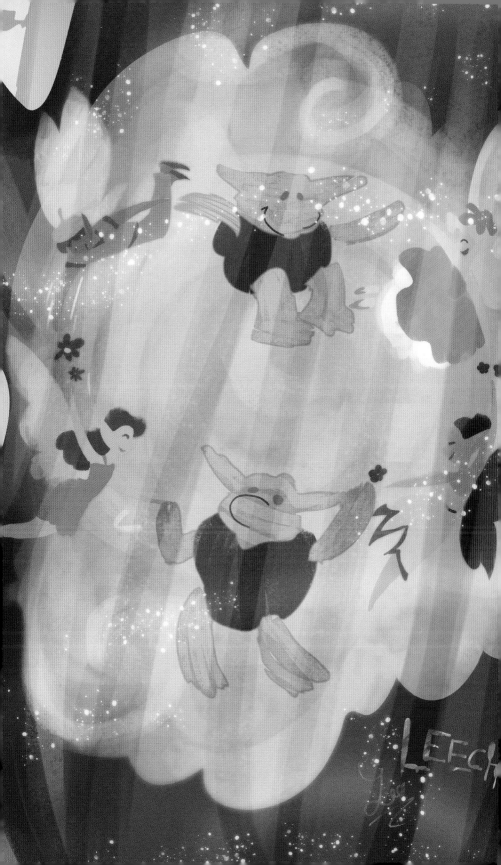